Cinderella

Adapted by Thea Feldman

Illustrated by the Disney Storybook Artists

A GOLDEN BOOK • NEW YORK

Copyright © 2012 Disney Enterprises, Inc. All rights reserved. Published in the United States by Golden Books, an imprint of Random House Children's Books, a division of Random House, Inc., 1745 Broadway, New York, NY 10019, and in Canada by Random House of Canada Limited, Toronto, in conjunction with Disney Enterprises, Inc. Golden Books, A Golden Book, A Big Golden Book, the G colophon, and the distinctive gold spine are registered trademarks of Random House, Inc.

ISBN: 978-0-7364-3002-9

randomhouse.com/kids

Printed in the United States of America

10 9 8 7 6 5 4 3 2 1

Once upon a time in a faraway land, a beautiful girl named Cinderella lived with her devoted father. Cinderella's mother had passed away years before, and her father decided she needed a new mother. He married again, giving Cinderella a stepmother and two stepsisters.

When Cinderella's father suddenly passed away, she was heartbroken. The poor girl quickly discovered that her stepmother, Lady Tremaine, was cold, cruel, and bitterly jealous of Cinderella's charm and beauty. Her stepsisters, Anastasia and Drizella, were equally cruel.

As the years passed, Cinderella became a servant in her own home. She was forced to live in a tiny room in the attic and had to wait on her stepfamily all day long. Luckily, Cinderella's animal friends kept her company.

Though her stepfamily mistreated her, Cinderella believed her dreams would come true someday. She remained kind and gentle, even sewing little clothes for her mice friends and making sure they were always safe and fed. Two of the mice, Jaq and Gus, became Cinderella's best friends.

One morning, poor Gus was almost caught by the Stepmother's mean old cat, Lucifer! Luckily, Gus managed to slip away and hide under a teacup on a breakfast tray.

Just as Lucifer was about to discover Gus's hiding place, a bell rang. That meant Lady Tremaine and her daughters wanted their breakfast. Balancing the trays, Cinderella hurried up the stairs, unaware that she was carrying a little stowaway under one of the teacups.

Shortly after breakfast was served, Cinderella heard screams. Anastasia had found Gus under her cup! She accused Cinderella of serving her a mouse on purpose!

Cinderella was immediately summoned back to Lady Tremaine's room. "As punishment," her stepmother said, "you will wash the windows, scrub the terrace, and sweep the halls."

Meanwhile, in another part of the kingdom, the King was complaining to the Grand Duke.

"It's time the Prince got married!" he declared.

The King decided to invite every eligible maiden to a royal ball so his son could find a bride.

Later that morning, Cinderella stopped doing her chores to answer a knock at the door. A messenger from the palace handed her an invitation to the ball that evening!

Lady Tremaine snatched the invitation and read it aloud. Her daughters squealed with excitement. When Cinderella asked if she could attend the ball, too, Lady Tremaine reluctantly agreed.

"But only if you get all your work done, and only if you have something suitable to wear," she said with a nasty sneer.

In the attic, Cinderella found a dress that had once belonged to her mother. It was a bit old-fashioned, but Cinderella was sure she could fix it.

Just as she was about to start sewing, her stepfamily called for her. There were many more chores to do. Cinderella sadly left the room—and her animal friends got right to work!

The clever animals found an old sash and some beads. They stitched the ornaments in place and turned the simple dress into a fabulous gown!

Cinderella was thrilled, and so grateful. Now she could go to the ball!

When Anastasia and Drizella saw how pretty Cinderella looked, they flew into a jealous rage. The stepsisters ripped the dress, pulled off the sash, and yanked at the beads. Lady Tremaine simply stood and watched.

With no hope of going to the ball and meeting the Prince,
Cinderella ran into the garden and sobbed.

As she kneeled there, twinkling lights filled the air. Then
a woman appeared. It was Cinderella's fairy godmother!

The Fairy Godmother told Cinderella there was still time to attend the royal ball. With a wave of her magic wand, she transformed a simple pumpkin into an elegant coach, and the mice into horses!

Then the Fairy Godmother pointed her magic
wand at Cinderella and said, "Bibbidi-bobbidi-boo!"
Suddenly, Cinderella was wearing a stunning gown.
On her feet were sparkling glass slippers.

Cinderella was off to the ball! The Fairy Godmother warned her to be home by midnight, when the spell would wear off.

At the ball, the Prince was introduced to all the eligible maidens in the kingdom. Anastasia and Drizella curtsied to him, but someone else caught the Prince's eye.

The Prince hurried over to the most beautiful girl he had ever seen. He and Cinderella danced all night without even introducing themselves. Cinderella had no idea she was dancing with the Prince! She was having the most wonderful night of her life—and then the clock began to chime midnight.

Cinderella had forgotten about the time! She ran down the palace steps, losing a glass slipper along the way.

"Wait! I don't know your name!" the Prince called.

The Grand Duke rushed after Cinderella, but she didn't stop.

Cinderella and her friends made it through the palace gates before the spell wore off and everything turned back to normal. Her beautiful dress was gone, but thanks to her fairy godmother, Cinderella still had the memories of an incredible evening—and one glass slipper!

Back at the palace, the King was furious that the girl his son wanted to marry had vanished. He ordered the Grand Duke to find her.

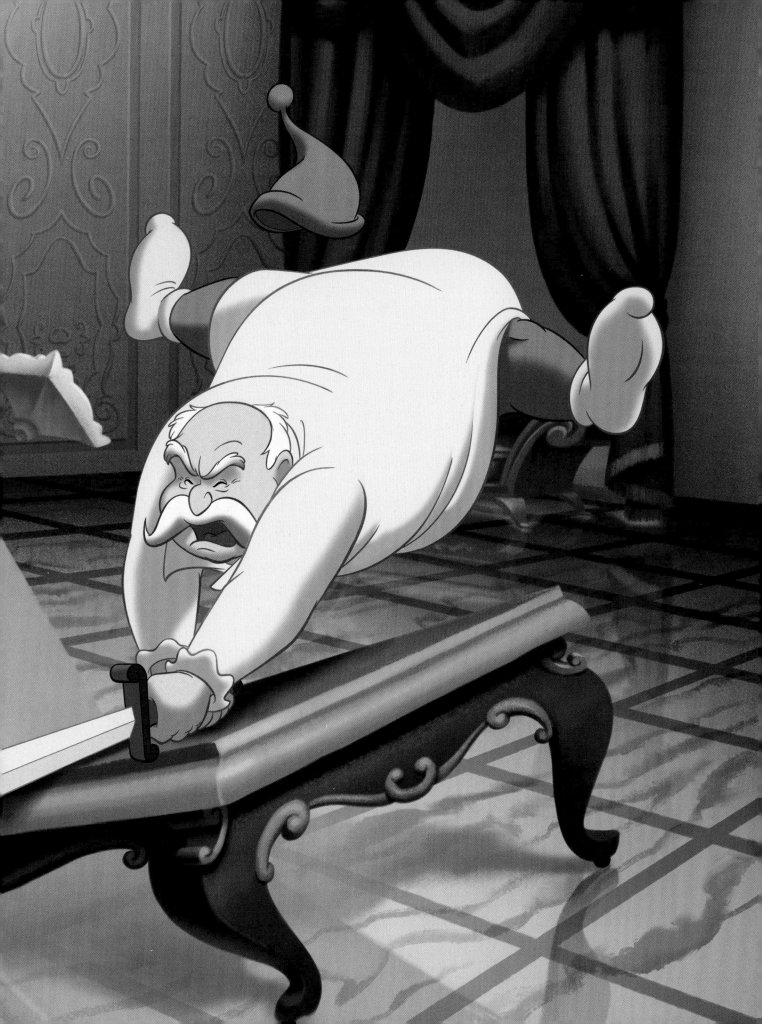

Word spread that the Prince was searching for the girl who had lost a glass slipper. Lady Tremaine suspected it was Cinderella but didn't know for certain. She didn't want Cinderella to have a chance to try on the shoe. She locked the poor girl in her room just before the Grand Duke arrived.

The Grand Duke explained that every maiden in the kingdom was to try on the slipper. The girl who fit the slipper perfectly would marry the Prince!

While Anastasia and Drizella tried to squeeze their big feet into the dainty slipper, Jaq and Gus stole the key to Cinderella's room from Lady Tremaine's pocket and unlocked the door. Cinderella rushed downstairs just as the Grand Duke was preparing to leave.

Lady Tremaine could not allow Cinderella to try on the shoe! She tripped the footman, causing the glass slipper to fall and shatter. But Cinderella surprised them all. She had the other slipper in her pocket. And, of course, it was a perfect fit!

Cinderella and the Prince were soon married, to the delight of the King. But no one was happier than Cinderella, whose dreams had come true at last!